CHANTICLEER

Henry Chafetz

CHANTICLEER

The Story of a Proud Rooster

❧

BASED ON THE PLAY CHANTECLER

BY EDMOND ROSTAND

WITH DRAWINGS BY ROBERT NADLER

PANTHEON BOOKS

To Helen, Michael, Eric, and Wayne
in the hope that no matter how violent the times
they will always show a dauntless courage
in devotion to truth.

CHANTICLEER

If you ever lived in France, you surely would know about Chanticleer, a rooster of great renown. There never was, and never ever again will be, any other rooster like him in France or anywhere else in the world.

Chanticleer was broad across his back and shoulders. He was also as handsome as he was strong. The comb on his proudly-held head was redder than the scarlet poppies that grow in the fields of France. His

bill was blacker than the most precious ebony from far-off Ceylon. The bright orange feathers on his head and neck faded to a pale golden color toward his back. Upon his chest there were feathers more golden than the gold of the sunflower. His upright tail was full, with long flowing feathers, partly green and partly black, that in the sunlight gleamed like precious jewels. His yellow-orange legs, upon which he stood proud and erect, were touched with blue. But the most wonderful thing about Chanticleer was his voice.

Every morning like a clock Chanticleer was the first in the land to awaken and to bring life to the world. His crowing was not just any ordinary *Co co ri co*. (In France all roosters crow *Co co ri co*. This is French for Cock-a-doodle-doo!) Chanticleer's call was more musical than the other roosters'. It was a song.

Chanticleer's song was as clear as it was loud. No creature within miles could fail to hear it, unless they had stones in their ears.

They heard it each morning in the valley.

They heard it in the forest.

3

They heard it in far-off towns, as daylight began to break the darkness.

Chanticleer's song echoed for miles across the countryside. And it seemed to echo and re-echo from the earth to the sky. Chanticleer was never hoarse in voice, nor was he ever out of breath.

While the daytime world was still fast asleep and morning still dark, Chanticleer stood alert and still like a statue. Then, the moment when the last gray mist of night was fleeing behind the sky, Chanticleer lifted his face upward, spread wide his wings, and called in his strong voice:

CO CO RI CO!
CO CO RI CO!
CO CO RI CO!

The night vanished as he sang, and the Dawn would begin to brighten the sky when his song was finished. And when Chanticleer saw the Dawn he beat his wings proudly in the air.

"When Chanticleer calls, day will surely come," all the fowls, animals, birds, and insects of the earth agreed. "His song is stronger than the night," they said.

Yet once more each morning, Chanticleer stood firmly on the ground, and facing eastward, lifted his head. Again, he crowed in a most powerful voice that reached to the sky.

CO CO RI CO!
CO CO RI CO!
CO CO RI CO!

When Chanticleer finished his song, he would again beat the air with his wings.

When he finished his song the Sun would begin to rise up over the eastern edge of the world. The Sun seemed to hear Chanticleer's sky-borne voice asking it to bring brightness and warmth and hope over the earth.

"Chanticleer knows the birthplace of the Sun. And when he calls, it will surely come," all the creatures of the land agreed.

When the Sun begins to climb above the land, the

world from earth to sky is made bright. Birds peek out of their nests and sing, as butterflies flutter and spread their wings. Leaves are fresh with dew, and flowers begin to bloom. Gentle breezes blow, as bumblebees, seeking honey, buzz their way to the flowers. And on the farm the dog barks, awakening the cat sleeping against the wall of the barn.

In the hen house, all the fowls open their eyes and begin their day. The chicks cheep, the hens cluck, and the young roosters crow happily. There are grains of corn in the feeding box and this is another day to walk in the sun. Unafraid, they can hunt and claw in the ground for worms. Chanticleer will not let any harm come to them.

They know Chanticleer stands ready to fight off hawks that snatch hen and chick away. Why, only the other day Chanticleer had rushed in and ripped off some of the feathers of the Great Hawk's wings just as the savage bird, silently hovering over the ground, was about to pounce upon an unsuspecting hen. And *caw-caw-cawing* in fright, the Hawk flew away into the safe distance of the sky. They know Chanticleer guards the hen house from hungry foxes and keeps safe from even the most sly and quick of weasels all the eggs laid by the mother hens.

Every morning Chanticleer strutted around the farm like a king, and under his careful eye there was no idleness.

Every morning he called to the ganders to lead the geese and goslings and the ducks and ducklings to the pond. And he ordered the turkeys to keep grasshoppers out of the cabbage beds and earth bugs off the wild carrots.

He made the young roosters practice their crowing, and the hens sit on their eggs. When he sent the roosters and chickens to chase the caterpillars away from the flowers, he told them to step carefully as they walked through the meadow.

"Young flowers are weak and crush easily," he warned.

Chanticleer even told the young roosters and chicks what to eat and why.

"Eat grains of corn and rye every day, and your feathers will be thick and shiny, your bodies strong and healthy."

Chanticleer was prouder than the eagles who fly high and make their nests at the very tops of mountains. In fact, Chanticleer believed he was more than ruler of the farmyard and guardian of the garden. He thought, as did all the farm creatures, that he was the greatest rooster that ever lived; for he and they believed that Dawn would not come unless Chanticleer called it with his unusually strong voice; and also, that if he should ever fail to call forth the Sun, it would not rise. If this ever happened, not only the countryside but the whole world would not, and perhaps would never again, behold the light of day.

"My song is a song of wonders," he told himself many times.

Chanticleer was full of kind thoughts for all who lived in the farmyard, and most of the farmyard creatures, big and small, admired and willingly obeyed Chanticleer and were his friends.

There were, however, some who were jealous of him, and there were also some who even hated him. Important as he was to the farmyard and great as he thought himself to the world, Chanticleer could not see beyond seeing that he was not liked by all.

Nor could he hear beyond hearing the many things said about him in secrecy by false friends.

The cat on the farm told a duck that Chanticleer was his enemy because the dog on the farm was Chanticleer's very good friend.

"I dislike him also, because he has no webbed feet," admitted the duck.

"His feet make star tracks wherever he walks on bare earth," a goose snickered.

A rooster who was scrawny and plain told an old turkey he had no liking for Chanticleer because he was too handsome.

This old turkey was jealous of Chanticleer. "I remember Chanticleer when he was young and no different than any growing rooster on the farm," the old turkey said scornfully. "No one would have thought that he would grow so big and that his voice would become so strong, and that he would be so famous."

The sightless mole, who lived under the earth where the ground is unpleasantly damp, came to the foot of the small mound of earth he had raised by burrowing underneath.

"I hate Chanticleer on principle!" he declared.

"Why?" asked the Blackbird.

"Because I never saw him," the mole answered.

The Blackbird was the most jealous of Chanticleer. The Blackbird knew how to whistle, but none of the creatures on the farm were impressed with his tunes. They all agreed Chanticleer's crowing was far superior. The Blackbird, who had once lived with some sparrows in Paris, the biggest city in France, thought he had seen everything and knew everything worth knowing. Too lazy to work, the Blackbird spent his time complaining about the simple life on the farm. He thought he was wiser than any other creature on the farm, wiser even than Chanticleer, who had never been away from the farm.

Chanticleer did not know that these things were said about him. He did not know either that there were those who hated him so much they wished to do him great harm. These were the creatures who by day had to be quiet with closed eyes, hidden from sight. Only in the night, when they came out to creep or fly, did their eyes open.

The owls and the bats, among the night creatures, especially hated Chanticleer. For did he not awaken the Dawn to chase the night away? Early every morning, when the first notes of Chanticleer's song were heard, they ran to hide themselves, for they were helpless and blind in the light of day. If they could only still Chanticleer, there would be darkness on the farm and all around on the hills and meadows, and their nighttime world would never end.

There would be more time for horned owls to catch sleeping partridges, barn owls to seize unsuspecting sleeping rabbits, and church owls to feast on mice and rats. Old owls, whose health was poor, would have all the hours they needed to search out, kill, and devour tender jays and doves and linnets. Owlets, too young to hunt and kill, could freely steal and eat the eggs they found in the nests of birds.

Yes, if they could only still Chanticleer . . .

One night, when the moon was hidden behind the clouds and no stars could be seen, all the night creatures held a great meeting to plan Chanticleer's death. The night was too dark and too gloomy for the noisy crickets to come out and sing and play, and even the leaves of the trees were silent.

That night, in the silent darkness, while the rest of the world slept, Chanticleer's enemies came to a hilltop beyond the farm, to the yew tree which stood in the center of a ring of holly trees.

There were night birds who flew high and night animals who crawled low. Bats zigzagged wildly to the meeting place and moles burrowed their way up the hill.

All of the owls were there too, hooting and screeching as they came, their yellow eyes gleaming in the dark as they waited for the meeting to begin. There were old owls and owlets, barn owls, church owls, great horned owls, hoot owls, screech owls and wood owls. The Cat from the farm and the Blackbird were there also. They came as representatives of Chanticleer's false friends in the farmyard. The Cat was crouched on the grass. Alongside the Cat was the Blackbird, who rested on a piece of dried and rotted wood. The Cat's eyes looked very green in the night and the Blackbird whistled excitedly.

Hundreds of fireflies formed ranks in a wide circle around the yew tree and gave off the only glow in the dark of the hilltop. Around them, but not too close, were the night creatures. Some squatted on the ground, some sat on the rocks, others crowded and clustered together on the limbs of the holly trees. Many bats hung face-down from the limbs of the holly trees. A number of bats who came late hovered overhead like dark shadows, beating the night air with their wings and squealing for the meeting to start. A very large Great Horned Owl, perched on a high branch of the yew tree, finally called the meeting to order.

"We all agree Chanticleer is a thief," he cried.

"Break him, body and bones!" the bats shrieked.

"Chanticleer steals the night away from us," the Great Horned Owl went on. "When his crowing calls the Dawn we must stop our hunting and killing and feasting, and we must hide and stay still as stones during the day."

"Destroy him, flesh, feathers, and blood!" all the owls screeched.

"Do we all agree then that Chanticleer must be killed?" the Great Horned Owl asked.

"It is absolutely necessary! Death to Chanticleer!" all present at the meeting screamed in approval.

"Idiots! Foolish talk! How may this be?" The old Great Horned Owl asked. "We of the night are blind in the day, and Chanticleer stirs only by day."

The Blackbird called out: "I have a plan. I will tell you how Chanticleer's death can be."

All eyes turned in the dark toward the Blackbird.

"Come forward then and let us hear," the Great Horned Owl commanded.

The Blackbird flew to the yew tree and stood on the branch alongside the Great Horned Owl.

"Chanticleer," he said, "is a rooster of might, but he is not a match for a genuine champion fighting cock whose ankles are armed with spurs of sharp steel that give deadly wounds."

The Blackbird paused and looked around at his audience. All were quiet; only their eyes blinked and gleamed in the darkness.

"I know such a fighting cock," declared the Blackbird. "He is truly ferocious. Even his name, Assassin,

has a deadly meaning. He lives only to maim and kill, and he will surely come to fight Chanticleer."

"But will he defeat and kill Chanticleer?" an old owl asked.

The Blackbird laughed before he answered.

"Assassin has slain many a fighting cock to earn his fame. He has never lost a match. With the spurs that are bound to his ankles he will break Chanticleer's wings. Then he will gouge out Chanticleer's eyes. And then, he will silence Chanticleer forever."

The creatures of the night gloated and swayed with glee. In their imaginations they saw Chanticleer lying on the ground with eyeless sockets and no life in his heart.

But suddenly fear struck them as the first notes of Chanticleer's call to the Dawn pierced their ears.

CO CO RI CO!

It was a hateful sound to the bats and the owls. Trembling and frightened, Chanticleer's night foes scattered wildly in all directions, fleeing to their dark hiding places as Dawn began to move up over the sky and earth. No one was left on the hilltop except the Blackbird and the Cat.

One afternoon, several days later, a strange rooster appeared and crowed lustily in front of the hen house. The Blackbird nudged the Cat with his wing as Chanticleer and all the other farm creatures hurried over to greet the visitor.

The crest and head of this rooster were orange-red and there were scars on his beak. His breast and tail were the color of silver, and his back and wings were crimson. The stranger's body was lean, but his legs were stout. His tail was small and carried low, and the feathers on his tail were short and hard. His beady eyes were as cold as ice and he glared as Chanticleer and the rest of the farm creatures flocked around him.

Chanticleer, who was most hospitable, stepped forward ceremoniously.

"Welcome," he said to the strange rooster. "What is your name? From what farm do you come?" he asked.

"Assassin is my name," the stranger answered in a voice most hard and unpleasant. "My home is everywhere that might is right, so I am always on the go," he said.

"We are just plain fowls here, but you are welcome to stay as long as you wish," said Chanticleer very politely.

"Where I go I seldom stay, but I'm never forgotten," Assassin replied. And then he strutted all around Chanticleer in a most insolent fashion.

Three times the rooster named Assassin strutted around Chanticleer. Suddenly he whirled about and stared at Chanticleer without saying a word.

"You are deliberately rude," declared Chanticleer, shocked by the stranger's behavior.

The rooster called Assassin stood with his feet spread apart. Fluttering his wings defiantly he sneered at Chanticleer.

"And you cackle like a hen," he said.

Chanticleer was quite indignant.

"I believe you do not know to whom you are speaking," he told Assassin. "I am Chanticleer! My song calls the Dawn. My song brings the Sun to the sky and light over the earth."

Chanticleer clawed the earth. Then he spread his wings very proudly and crowed very loudly.

"Fine feathers and loud crowing do not always make a cock great," Assassin replied disdainfully. "My reputation is measured by the roosters I have fought and killed. I'm fast as lightning and there is death in my blows," he bragged, scratching the grass with his claws.

Chanticleer was quite annoyed as well as bewildered. He knew no reason for the stranger to be angry with him.

"You crow your own praise and you seek a quarrel without reason," he said.

"I come not unbidden, and I will not leave until we have fought," declared Assassin.

"I have protected and I have helped. Who would ask you to come? Who would want to see me dead?" Chanticleer asked.

"Many want your death," replied Assassin.

"Who? Why?" Chanticleer asked, not believing his ears.

"I do not care who or why, I care only to fight and to prove I am greater than you," said Assassin.

Assassin's speech chilled the blood of Chanticleer's friends, but delighted his enemies.

"The stranger is a fighter, every inch of him," the Cat purred admiringly and licked her paws in delight.

"It is a challenge!" the Blackbird whistled aloud.

"A challenge!" cried all of Chanticleer's false friends.

"A challenge! A challenge!" all the chickens cackled.

"Chanticleer must fight!" the ducks quacked excitedly.

"A fight!" the geese honked.

There was wild excitement. Every creature on the farm except the hogs gathered to witness the fight. They were too busy eating to know what was going on.

"Form a circle around them," a turkey called out.

Everyone immediately moved back and formed

a wide ring several rows deep around Chanticleer and Assassin. Those who were too far in the rear climbed onto the hen house and the fence, the better to see the two roosters fight.

Chanticleer knew he had to fight the stranger or be called a coward. If he fought and lost, he would be humiliated. He might also be killed, for Assassin seemed to be no ordinary fighting cock. But Chanticleer was as strong in courage as he was in voice. Ready to fight, he stood face to face with Assassin.

The Blackbird whistled a signal and the fight began.

Chanticleer and Assassin flew at each other double-quick. They parried and thrust, and each warded off the other's blows. The roosters seemed evenly matched.

The spectators clucked and chattered.

"Assassin's fast and nimble."

"He's a sensation!"

They stamped their feet and cheered with delight when Assassin, with a sudden fierce blow, made Chanticleer reel and stagger back.

These were hateful sounds for Chanticleer to hear.

"How can this be?" he asked himself.

The excited faces of many whom he thought were his friends and admirers eagerly waiting for him to be killed revealed to Chanticleer what long had been hid. Sad of heart, he knew now what Assassin meant when he said he had not come unbidden. Chanticleer felt betrayed, but he continued to fight in defense of his honor.

Hidden under the feathers of Assassin's legs were a pair of steel spurs fixed to his ankles, the razor-sharp, pointed type worn by professional killer cocks. Now the spurs came to sight as Assassin savagely and grimly flew and thrust and thrust and flew feet first at Chanticleer.

Chanticleer dodged the spurs as best as he could, but suddenly Assassin stabbed him in the neck. Chanticleer fell back.

"He's wounded!" the spectators shouted.

Then Assassin struck Chanticleer in the eye with the other spur.

"He bleeds!" the crowd shouted deliriously.

Blinded by his own blood and painfully sore, Chanticleer was easily knocked down. But even as

he lay on his back he defended himself by kicking back at Assassin's spurred feet. He uttered not a plea for mercy, not a word of surrender. His eyes, however, were full of tears; not for the pain he felt, but for the cheers of the spectators for Assassin.

The fight was unfair. Chanticleer, unarmed, was helpless against Assassin's steel spurs. Each time he fought back, Chanticleer had less strength to continue, and his blows became weaker.

Chanticleer began to roll over.

"He's hardly alive!" exclaimed Chanticleer's enemies. They clapped their hands and cried, "Hooray for Assassin!"

Chanticleer's few loyal friends pleaded for the fight to stop. But their cries were drowned out by the applause and excited shouts of the other spectators.

Assassin's sharp spurs stabbed at Chanticleer again and again. Assassin jumped into the air for the final thrust, but Chanticleer managed to roll aside just in time and Assassin's spurred feet landed on empty ground.

Chanticleer now lay back and waited with closed

eyes. Assassin would not miss this time. But the expected blows did not come, and the cheering for Assassin had stopped.

Surprised, Chanticleer lifted his head and looked around. The spectators, their eyes raised to the sky, were pale and speechless and trembling with fear. Assassin was running to a hedge, where he crouched low and hid his head under his own wings. All the chickens and ducks and geese and turkeys began to run to Chanticleer, as a hawk, whose great pair of wings made a giant shadow on the earth, passed over them.

The Hawk was the common enemy, and Chanticleer was the protector of the farmyard. Chanticleer knew what he had to do, and he did it quickly.

Even though he was wounded and exhausted and bleeding in many places, Chanticleer found the strength to rise from the ground. It was a noble sight as Chanticleer managed to stand as tall as he could.

"Come closer to me, all of you," he commanded as he often had in the past.

And all the fowls, moaning with fear, their heads bent low between their wings, came as close as

31

possible to Chanticleer. Assassin cowered low along-side the hedge as the Hawk circled again, this time closer to the frightened fowls.

Some incubator chicks who had no mother hens' wings to protect them, ran under Chanticleer's wings. Just in time, too, for the Hawk was now close above them. It circled again, ready to dart down and seize a victim.

As the shadow of the Hawk spread like a dark shape overhead, Chanticleer called out in a warning voice: "Hawk! I am still here!"

At the sound of Chanticleer's voice, the Hawk flew quickly away. All the fowls cried for joy at being saved. Chanticleer felt a new strength.

Chanticleer's few true friends rejoiced, but their joy was short. The feathered creatures of the farm, eager for the fight to continue, formed into a circle again.

"Can they so quickly forget they trembled for their lives and were saved by you from the Hawk?" his friends asked Chanticleer.

"They have made no secret of their dislike for me. They wish to see me killed," Chanticleer replied in a grieved voice. "But no fear. I will defeat Assassin now," he declared.

Chanticleer strode over to Assassin who still stood by the hedge.

"The Hawk's shadow made you lose courage, and now it shall be you who falls in fight," he told Assassin.

The killer cock was surprised by Chanticleer's new strength. He was also puzzled.

"Why did you deliver from danger those whose envy and hate is strong enough to want your death?" he asked Chanticleer. "They will always envy and hate you," he said.

"Why must that be so?" Chanticleer wished to know.

"Because you are without fear, and because you have seen the fear in their eyes," Assassin replied.

"Speak what you will, but now we must finish the fight," declared Chanticleer.

No sooner had Chanticleer spoken than Assassin flew at him, both spurs exposed, in a surprise attack. Chanticleer, however, leaped aside, and as Assassin landed on the ground, the spur on one of his legs accidently stabbed his other leg. Assassin fell in pain, wounded by his own spur.

The cheers of the spectators for Assassin now turned to jeers.

"Kill the stranger!" they urged Chanticleer.

"Kill! Kill! Kill!" they whistled and clucked and chanted. "Kill! Kill! Kill!"

Chanticleer looked at them scornfully.

"It is foolish to hate without good cause, and there is not true reason to kill. Leave!" he commanded Assassin.

Crippled and in pain, but happy to be alive, Assassin rose to his feet. His head hanging low, he limped away in disgrace. The fickle fowls, who only a short time before had cheered him as their champion, booed and called Assassin all sorts of ugly names as he left the farm.

Chanticleer's real friends came up and congratulated him for defeating Assassin.

"I thank you for your loyalty," he said to them.

Then all those who had encouraged Assassin came in a crowd, cheering Chanticleer.

"No closer, not one of you! Save your clapping

35

and flapping for another Assassin," Chanticleer shouted at them.

All the fowls stopped and moved backward a few steps.

Chanticleer's heart was choked with fury, but he did not think long about what he had to say.

"You change leaders and heroes too quickly. By your action today, you have named yourselves false friends to me."

Chanticleer took a deep breath and in a heavy voice continued. "I will go my own way now. I do not want to see any of you again."

"Why must you leave us? And where will you go?" his friends asked Chanticleer.

"I have lost faith in my fellow creatures. The song has gone out of me, and I feel I am no longer of use. I shall make the nearby forest my home," he told his friends.

"All sorts of wild beasts make their home in the woods," they warned Chanticleer.

"But even wild beasts are less false," he replied.

Sadly, they watched as Chanticleer turned away toward the forest.

Chanticleer entered the forest and wandered among the trees until he came to a brook. Dipping his beak into the water he drank until he was full. Then he sat down wearily on the fallen leaves in front of a giant oak tree.

The hour had grown late and the shadows of early darkness had just begun to deepen. All he could see were the tops of the trees. Chanticleer had never been in the forest before, and it was quite strange to him to look up and not see the sky.

Chanticleer sighed to himself. What could he do now but live alone in the forest? He looked about him. Nearby, a cluster of mushrooms, like houses in a village, grew.

While he was resting, Chanticleer heard low croaking sounds. Out of the mossy banks of the brook there hopped a group of toads. They hopped together in a row until they came near Chanticleer. Then, each

of the toads hopped alongside a mushroom and peered at Chanticleer.

Rubbing their warty noses and bowing their knobby heads they spoke. "Welcome to the forest."

"Please sit down," Chanticleer told them politely.

At that, each of the toads hopped right atop the mushroom next to it. Without blinking their bulging eyes, and with no hesitation they said, "Word was received of your arrival, and we are the committee chosen from amongst all the toads to ask you to become the new Voice of the Forest."

Chanticleer was as surprised as he was flattered. He stood erect and asked, "Is there an old Voice of the Forest?"

"The nightingale, a little bird," replied one toad.

"With a weak voice," said another toad.

"The nightingale's voice, which sends no echoes, cannot be compared to yours. Why! Your voice, powerful in tone, reaches even the forest at dawn," a third toad declared.

"It is true that I have a strong voice," said Chanticleer with pride. "But what kind of a song does this little nightingale sing?"

"Your song puts the nightingale's to shame," replied a fourth toad. "We wish a change."

"Something different! Something new! A song with range!" exclaimed the first toad.

"Change! Range! Hooray for Chanticleer, Cock of the Dawn! The new Voice of the Forest!" all the toads croaked loudly.

Chanticleer was quite impressed, for they spoke to him as if he were the most important creature in the whole forest. He considered their words.

If what the toads told him was true, the nightingale's voice must be counted weak, and there could be no doubt that he had the greater song. The welcoming committee of toads did seem very serious and quite positive. Who better than himself to be the new Voice of the Forest? No weak voice, surely, could call the Dawn and summon the Sun.

Farmyard or forest, what did it matter where he sang? Chanticleer could not forget how the farmyard fowls had cheered for Assassin. But now, he began to feel that life was not always unkind. Here in the forest he had found creatures who admired him for what he could do.

Chanticleer did not think long to give the toads an answer. Clapping his wings he said, "I will crow for you in a voice that will shatter the air and carry my song even beyond the forest."

"Long live Chanticleer!" the toads croaked in accord.

"But I must go to sleep now," Chanticleer told the toads. "When I awake I will bring the Dawn and the Sun with a voice you will never forget."

The toads offered Chanticleer rainworms to eat (really wholesome food for roosters), while they ordered the spiders to weave a blanket bed of silky cobweb threads for him in the hollow of the trunk of the giant oak tree.

"We will sleep atop the mushrooms, for we wish to hear you sing when you awake," the toads told Chanticleer.

When the spiders were finished with their task Chanticleer said goodnight to the toads and disappeared into the hollow of the tree. He fell asleep, happy again.

It was not yet time for Chanticleer to rise and call the Dawn, when a small voice, clear and true and

soft, woke him from his sleep. Chanticleer listened in awe.

He stepped out from the hollow of the tree. His heart quickened many a beat and his face became still as a mask as the song, silver-clear, called from overhead nearby in the forest. It was a long slow song that began low and rose higher and higher with each note. A hush came over the forest as the last note soared upward into the air like a tinkle of sound that could barely be heard.

Oh-h-h holeee holeee . . .
Ah-h-h pure itteee pure itteee . . .
Eee sweet-sweet sweetleee . . .

"Perfect! Never have I heard anything so beautiful in all my life," Chanticleer sighed, and all the feathers of his crest shook with delight as the song came forth again.

"What marvelous voice sings?" he asked the toads, who had awakened during the song.

"The-the-the Nightingale," one of the toads stammered in a low embarrassed voice.

45

Chanticleer became enraged and shook his wings furiously at the toads.

"You lied to me," he cried. "You dared to poison me against *that* little bird? The Nightingale's song should sound your shame for the unjust words you have said about it."

Chanticleer was also angry at himself. It made him grieve to think he had believed the toads.

"You had me thinking things that were not true," he told the toads. "I see now that you wish to do to the Nightingale what the farmyard fowls did to me. How could you ever compare my rough voice to that of the Nightingale? Next to its song, mine is only loud make-believe. And I," he exclaimed, "how could I ever think I was greater than a bird I neither knew nor heard sing before?"

Eyeing the toads with great scorn, Chanticleer flapped his wings fiercely at them and chased them away.

As the toads hopped into the weeds and disappeared, the Nightingale sang again.

Oh-h-h holeee holeee . . .

Chanticleer looked to see where the song came from.

By now, the moon had paled and morning was near. Chanticleer could see the Nightingale poised on the branch of a tree. The bird's head was turned upward to the sky as it sang.

Ah-h-h pure itteee pure itteee . . .

Chanticleer stood and listened as the Dawn began to brighten the sky. Nearby, some rabbits popped out of their holes in the ground and lifted their long ears and listened with Chanticleer until the Nightingale finished its song.

Eee sweet-sweet sweetleee . . .

"Nightingale," Chanticleer called up to the bird. "There is nothing real, only your song. What it means I do not know, but this is true: more lies beyond your song than mine."

The Nightingale looked down and answered Chanticleer.

"There are no words to my song. What it means, all may not know. To some, it is a lullaby to the night. To others, it is anything those who listen to it wish to hear within themselves: new hope as old hope dies, truth, and faith in truth."

"It is pure music, and you sing as if you sing for the world," murmured Chanticleer.

"I only sing the song I know," the Nightingale replied.

It began to sing again.

Oh-h-h holeee hol—

Just then, a hunter's gun rang out, and the song stopped as the little Nightingale fell dead to the ground.

"Why do men shoot when they hear a song?" Chanticleer cried.

Gently he covered the unmoving body of the Nightingale with grass.

"The most valued voice in the world, gone. Who will sing its song now?" Sadly he bowed his head under his wings.

Oh-h-h holeee holeee . . .
Ah-h-h pure itteee pure itteee . . .
Eee sweet-sweet sweetlee . . .

Chanticleer looked up when he heard the same song. It was another nightingale in a tree right above him. And its voice was just as sweet and soft and pure as the nightingale whose little body, its voice hushed forever, lay still under the grass near Chanticleer's feet.

Even a rooster can think wisely. Chanticleer understood that in the forest there would always be a nightingale to sing. It was a victory over bullets and envy.

By now, the sky showed blue and it was morning. Chanticleer had been so enchanted by the Nightingale's singing that he had not noticed the changing skies and sung his own song. In the eastern sky, the bright glow of the Sun began to appear over the horizon. Now Chanticleer realized that it was not his voice that magically called the Dawn and the Sun daily. But Chanticleer was not sad, only wiser.

"I will never *Co co ri co* again, now that I have

heard your song," he told the Nightingale in the tree above him.

Shaking its head, the Nightingale spoke gently to Chanticleer.

"Nightingales and roosters may die, but our song and your crowing is never ended. Ours is a song of faith, yours is a cry for life. I must sing, you must crow. All the world needs our voices."

"But why should some hate our voices?" asked Chanticleer.

"There will always be toads and others who do not understand our songs, or why we sing," answered the Nightingale.

"All the words you say are wise," declared Chanticleer. Suddenly he wanted to sing again. "I will never again be sad of living or weary of crowing. My mind is clear. I will return to my own. Even if some cannot understand why, I will be at the service of the farmyard fowls. I know now it is my task, not to call the Dawn and the Sun, but to tell the world that it is morning and time to wake up and live."

Without a pause, without looking back, Chanticleer left the forest. Again and again he spread his wings and crowed aloud as he hurried, hopped, and flew back toward the farm.

CO CO RI CO!
CO CO RI CO!
CO CO RI CO!

The farmyard fowls, fearful since he had gone, were now happy to hear Chanticleer's voice in the distance. Joyfully they awaited his return.